The California GOLD★RUSH

Written by Pam Zollman

STECK-VAUGHN
ELEMENTARY · SECONDARY · ADULT · LIBRARY

A Harcourt Company

www.steck-vaughn.com

CONTENTS

CHAPTER 1

THE PEBBLE THAT CHANGED HISTORY

Gold! The word excites people. In their mind they see the yellow metal that shines like the sun. People have valued gold for thousands of years because it is beautiful and hard to find. Gold is the softest of the metals and can easily be shaped into jewelry and coins. It does not rust or lose its shine.

Because people value gold, they have spent a great deal of time and energy looking for it. When Spanish explorers came to the New World, some were looking for a kingdom of gold called El Dorado. Stories of El Dorado told of a place where sand of pure gold lay all around. Other Spanish explorers looked for seven gold cities called the Seven Cities of Cibola.

No one ever found El Dorado or the Seven Cities of Cibola, but one man did find gold in North America. His name was James Marshall, and he found the gold by accident.

James Marshall worked for John Sutter. Sutter was a wealthy man who owned 50,000 acres (5000 hectares) of land in California. In the early 1840s, he built Sutter's Fort on the American River. In 1847 he decided he wanted to build a sawmill at Coloma, a place near the point where the American River meets the Sacramento River. The fast-moving water would provide the force needed for sawing lumber. In August 1847, Sutter put James Marshall in charge of his sawmill project. On January 24, 1848, when the sawmill was almost finished, gold was discovered.

Jennie Wimmer cooked and washed for Marshall's sawmill crew. She claimed that her son, John, actually found the first **nugget**. However, most **historians** give the credit to James Marshall. Marshall said that he noticed something shiny in the water-flow channel at the mill. He picked up the small yellow pebble and compared it to a gold coin. He showed the pebble to Jennie Wimmer, who was making soap. Back then, people used lye, a very harsh chemical, to make soap. Wimmer knew that lye does not harm gold. She tossed the pebble into the lye kettle. The next morning, she plucked the pebble from the kettle. The lye hadn't hurt it at all. It was still shiny yellow.

James Marshall raced to Sutter's Fort to show Sutter what he'd found. Sutter then looked in books to find information about gold. He and Marshall weighed the pebble, and they put acid on it. The pebble was gold!

Sutter hurried to his sawmill. By then Wimmer's children had found about 4 more ounces (113 grams) of gold. Other members of the sawmill crew showed Sutter flakes and nuggets that they had collected.

John Sutter

All of them wondered whether they had found real gold. To find out, some of the men bit the nuggets. Others hit the nuggets with a hammer.

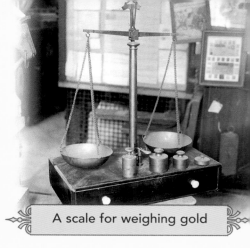

A scale for weighing gold

The nuggets bent, but they did not break.

Gold is a soft metal, but it is very sturdy. If the pebbles had flaked, they would have been pyrite, not gold. Pyrite is a common mineral that is also called fool's gold because it fools many people into thinking it's real gold.

Sutter began to worry. He was afraid that all the sawmill workers would leave to go look for gold. Then his sawmill would never get finished. If his workers at Sutter's Fort found out, they might leave to search for gold, too. Then his spring planting wouldn't get done. No one would care for his fields and herds of cattle. If other people heard about the gold, they'd swarm across his land.

Sutter asked Marshall and the sawmill crew to keep quiet about the gold, but the find was too important to keep secret. Some of the sawmill crew talked about it.

Visitors to the sawmill saw it themselves. More people found gold in other places along the American River. Even Sutter himself couldn't keep quiet about the discovery. He bragged to his friends about the gold found on his land.

Telegraphs did not reach to the West in 1848, and telephones did not exist. There were no radios or televisions or even daily mail service. Letters sometimes took months to arrive. The railroads didn't reach as far west as California yet. News of the California gold spread to nearby areas by word of mouth.

At first people didn't believe the stories about the gold. After all, there had been tall tales about gold for hundreds of years. But as more and more people found gold, the news spread rapidly. John Sutter's workers began to search for gold on their own.

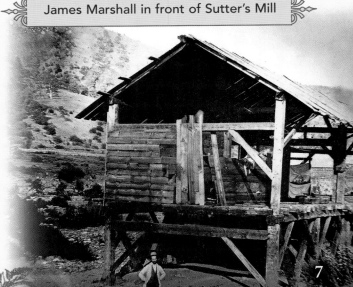
James Marshall in front of Sutter's Mill

Half the people who lived in nearby Monterey, California, also left to go to the **diggings**. That's what they called the mountain streams, rivers, and **gullies** where they looked for gold. Soon the blacksmith had the only Monterey business still open. He couldn't keep up with the need for pans, shovels, and picks.

In early 1848 San Francisco was a sleepy little town. Then in April of that year, people started going to San Francisco with bags full of gold to pay for things. While they were there, they spread the news about how easy it was to find gold. Sam Brannan was a newspaper publisher in San Francisco. He wondered if the stories of finding gold were true. He decided to see for himself, so he went to the diggings. On May 12, 1848, he walked through the streets of San Francisco, holding up a bottle of gold dust. "Gold!" he shouted. "Gold from the American River!" By May 19, 1848, the first large group of **prospectors** from San Francisco arrived at Sutter's Mill to look for gold.

Sam Brannan

In the summer of 1848, California was a **territory** of the United States. It wasn't a real state yet, but the land belonged to the United States. The United States received the land from Mexico on February 2, 1848—nine days after gold was discovered at Sutter's Mill. Mexico sold California as part of a **treaty** that ended the Mexican-American War. At that time Mexico didn't think that California was worth much. The United States didn't think so either. Neither country knew about the gold in California.

The United States made Richard Mason the head of government in California. In August 1848, Mason visited a gold camp on the American River. He filled an empty tea tin with gold dust and sent it to the President of the United States. It took four months for that tea tin to travel by ship from California to the east coast of North America. When the gold arrived in Washington, D.C., President James K. Polk put it on display for all to see. The **Gold Rush** was about to begin.

BRITISH NORTH AMERICA

Oregon Territory

California

Land bought from Mexico in February 1848

New Hampshire
Vermont
Maine
New York
Mass.
Rhode I.
Connecticut
New Jersey
Delaware
Maryland

Wisconsin
Michigan
Iowa
Illinois
Indiana
Ohio
Pennsylvania
Missouri
Kentucky
Virginia
Arkansas
Tennessee
North Carolina
South Carolina
Mississippi
Alabama
Georgia
Louisiana
Florida

Texas

MEXICO

Gulf of Mexico

ATLANTIC OCEAN

PACIFIC OCEAN

N

0   200   400   600 miles
0   200   400   600 kilometers

CHAPTER 2

GOLD FEVER !

By January 1849 newspapers all over the United States were running stories about California's gold. People all across the country dreamed about going to California and becoming rich. Newspapers were filled with ads for mining tools and tickets for traveling by ship. One newspaper ad showed a special California gold grease. Users were supposed to rub this grease all over their body and then roll down a hill. Only gold would stick to their skin. Many foolish people fell for this ad. They paid $10 for a box of worthless grease!

Wild stories began to spread by word of mouth. One rumor claimed that gold nuggets stuck to the roots of plants. All a person had to do was pull up plants and pluck off the gold. Another story said that all of California's streams and rivers were filled with gold. People also thought that they could pick up gold nuggets off the ground, just like picking up nuts.

Men who had been doctors, lawyers, carpenters, bankers, and teachers left those jobs. Farmers left their fields and animals. All dropped what they were doing and headed to California by the tens of thousands. Many left wives and children behind. They promised to bring back pocketfuls of gold. Meanwhile the women had to find other ways of making money to live.

Everyone was in a hurry to get to the gold, but in 1849 a person had only two ways to get to California. Traveling over land was one way. Railroads in North America didn't reach to California yet. People in the eastern United States who wanted to make the overland trip had to go by **wagon train**. All their belongings had to fit in a wagon only 9 feet long by 5 feet wide (2.7 meters by 1.5 meters). A heavy cloth cover kept out rain and snow.

Many wagon trains began the overland trip in Independence, Missouri. People used oxen or mules to pull the covered wagons. Oxen were sturdy and could go for long distances without water. Mules were faster, so people in a hurry used them to make the trip. Even so, most wagon trains only traveled about 20 miles (32 kilometers) a day.

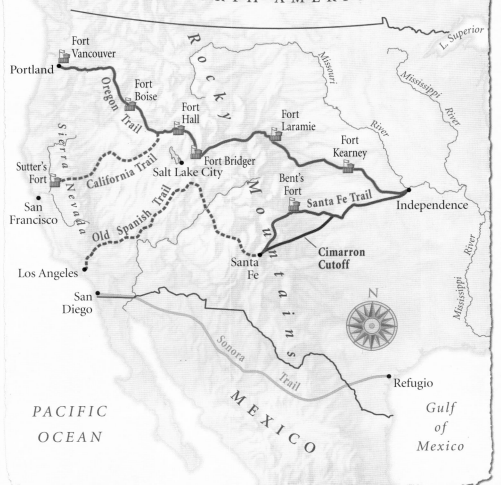

OVERLAND ROUTES TO CALIFORNIA

0   200   400   600 miles
0   200   400   600 kilometers

BRITISH NORTH AMERICA

L. Superior

Rocky

Missouri

Mississippi River

River

Fort Vancouver

Portland

Oregon Trail

Fort Boise

Fort Hall

Sierra Nevada

California Trail

Sutter's Fort

Salt Lake City

Fort Bridger

Fort Laramie

Fort Kearney

Bent's Fort

Santa Fe Trail

Independence

San Francisco

Old Spanish Trail

M o u n t a i n s

Los Angeles

Santa Fe

Cimarron Cutoff

San Diego

N

Mississippi River

Sonora Trail

MEXICO

Refugio

PACIFIC OCEAN

Gulf of Mexico

Most people thought that traveling by land to California was cheaper than going by ship, but it was not. Four people traveling together in one wagon spent $600 to $700 to outfit themselves for the trip. Once on the trail, they trudged through rainstorms, mud, sand, and snow. They went over mountains and through rivers. Some went without water and ate stale food.

Few women and children traveled to California during the Gold Rush, but young Sallie Hester did. She traveled by wagon train with her family. One day they passed through a canyon called Devil's Gate. The Sweetwater River cut through the canyon, and Sallie and some other children decided to go exploring. Sallie later wrote, "We made our way to the very edge of the cliff and looked down. We could hear the water dashing, splashing, and roaring as if angry at the small space through which it was forced to pass. We were gone so long that the train was stopped and men sent out in search of us. We made all sorts of promises to remain in sight in the future."

Sallie and the other children were lucky. Some people got lost on the way to California and were never found. Others got sick and died. Mules and oxen died from

A team of mules pulling a wagon on a mountain road in California

eating bad grass and left their owners with no way to pull their wagon. Some people became discouraged and went back home.

An overland trip to California took six to eight months. Ship captains promised a faster trip. Sailing from New York, around Cape Horn in South America, and then to San Francisco took five to seven months and cost from $100 to $300. Crossing over a narrow strip of land in Panama shortened the trip to weeks instead of months. Passengers traveled by canoe and mule across Panama to the Pacific coast, and then caught a ship sailing to San Francisco. They paid $200 to $400 for this trip.

Like overland travelers, passengers on ships faced many hardships. Food often rotted or became moldy.

If the wind did not blow, the ships went nowhere. If a storm blew up, the ships were hit by terrible winds, hard rain, and pounding waves. Travelers through Panama often came down with diseases such as malaria. They had to watch out for snakes and other wild animals on the slippery trails. They also had to battle mosquitoes and the heat of the jungle.

People who traveled through Panama had to make part of the trip by boat.

NORTH AMERICA

San Francisco

New York

ATLANTIC OCEAN

MEXICO

Gulf of Mexico

Panama City

PACIFIC OCEAN

SOUTH AMERICA

N

1,000   2,000 miles
1,000   2,000 kilometers

Cape Horn

CHAPTER 3

THE FORTY-NINERS

The year 1849 changed North America's history. In that year the first of about 300,000 people from all over the world began to hurry to California to look for gold. The rush included so many people that it was called the Gold Rush. The newspapers called the Gold Rush people **forty-niners** because that year was so important to the growth of California. No matter whether they came in 1849 or the following years, all the Gold Rush people were called forty-niners.

People who traveled by sea to reach California ended their voyage in San Francisco. In 1848 San Francisco was a town of about a thousand people. By the summer of 1849, San Francisco had grown to a city of almost 30,000. Hundreds of ships crowded San Francisco's harbor. Because many passengers and ship crews raced to the gold fields, ships were left empty in the harbor, where they rotted.

San Francisco in 1849

The few hotels in San Francisco were very **expensive**. Many people just pitched tents. Some dragged the empty ships ashore and used the wood to make buildings.

During the day, San Francisco looked dirty. Dust from the streets filled the air. Trash littered the walkways. At night, though, lantern light shone through the tents. It gave the whole city a soft golden glow.

Even though San Francisco was growing, many businesses closed at first. Their owners had taken off for the diggings. When forty-niners needing supplies flooded San Francisco, prices skyrocketed because the supply for goods could not keep up with the demand. Eggs cost $10 per dozen. Flour was $50 per barrel.

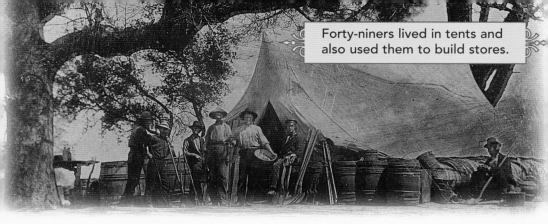

Forty-niners lived in tents and also used them to build stores.

A pick or shovel cost $10. One forty-niner recorded in his diary that he spent $11 for a jar of pickles and two sweet potatoes. Another gold seeker paid $43 for a box of sardines, a pound of hard bread, a pound of butter, and a half-pound of cheese. To pay for supplies, people often used gold dust and gold nuggets instead of money. They weighed the dust and nuggets to determine their value.

Most of the forty-niners were men in a hurry to get to the gold fields, the places where gold might be found. They didn't take time to plan how they'd live once they arrived. Most knew little or nothing about looking for gold. Some of the prospectors didn't take time to build houses or cabins. Instead they built lean-tos, or bush houses, by piling bushes and limbs together to form a shelter. Some used tents or lived in their covered wagon. Others built shacks from the wood in the wagons. Some even slept in holes in the ground.

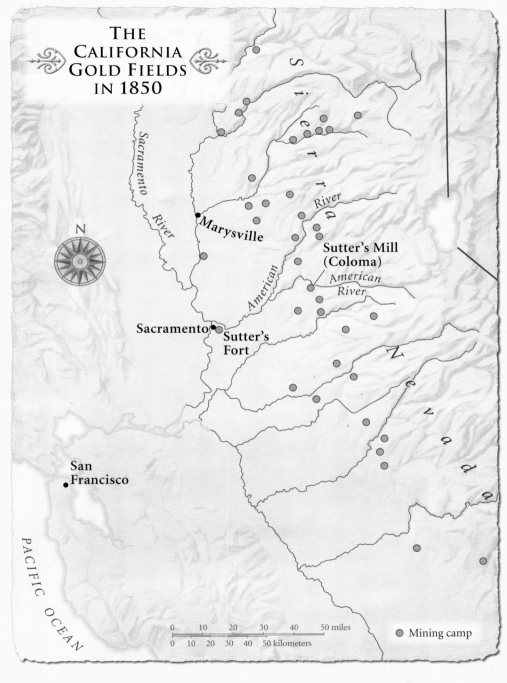

THE CALIFORNIA GOLD FIELDS IN 1850

Sacramento River

Sierra

River

N

Marysville

American River

Sutter's Mill (Coloma)

American River

Sacramento

Sutter's Fort

Nevada

San Francisco

PACIFIC OCEAN

| 0 | 10 | 20 | 30 | 40 | 50 miles |
| 0 | 10 | 20 | 30 | 40 | 50 kilometers |

● Mining camp

When a man reached the diggings, he drove wooden stakes into the ground to mark his **claim**. This way of marking a spot was called "staking a claim." If the man wanted to move to better diggings, he "pulled up stakes." A claim-jumper was a person who said a piece of staked land was his when it really wasn't. Prospectors worried about claim-jumpers and tried to mark their claim in a special way. For example, some decorated their stakes with tin cans or antlers.

Having a claim only meant that a person could look for gold on the land. It didn't mean that the person owned the land. If no gold was found or if all of it had been found, the prospector just went looking for another claim.

Several claims next to each other formed a mining camp, where people from all over the world worked side by side. African-American slaves brought to California could earn enough money to buy their freedom. They mined gold alongside American Indians and people from places such as England, Ireland, France, China, Australia, Mexico, and South America.

Prospectors often named their camps strange and funny names. Git Up and Git was a real place. So were

Hog Eye, Bogus Thunder, Mad Mule Gulch, and Lousy Ravine. The camps made their own rules because they were so far from judges and courts. Many forty-niners called the camp rules "the prospector's code." Some camps had rules about the size of a claim. These rules stated that a prospector could claim only as much land along a river as he could dig. In some places this area was only 100 square feet (9 square meters). People caught stealing could be whipped, have their head shaved, or have their cheeks branded. Prospectors often paid men called claims officers to guard their mining spot and to settle arguments.

Life in a mining camp

23

The forty-niners found that mining for gold was hard work. Their day began at dawn with a breakfast of coffee and hard biscuits. They then spent 10 to 12 hours looking for gold. The sun burned their neck and back. Once in a while, a lucky miner might find a gold nugget in a stream, river, or gully. Or he might find a handful of gold dust in a crevice between rocks. For most of the miners, though, looking for gold meant backbreaking work that required them to separate gold dust and flakes from tons of sand and gravel. In the eastern United States, $1 a day was good pay for a day's work. The average prospector might earn $15 per day

Prospectors lined the banks of many California rivers.

in California, but he might earn nothing. And he might earn nothing for days.

At dusk the prospectors went back to their tent or lean-to. For supper they'd eat some dried beef or pickled pork and drink more coffee. If they were lucky, they ate beans or potatoes with the meat. After supper many went straight to bed, too tired to stay awake any longer.

In their spare time, many prospectors wrote letters to tell their family about their experiences. Others took up boxing and wrestling. On Sundays the prospectors held foot races with cash prizes. Bowling and chess were popular, too. Many prospectors played cards for money or gold dust. Telling stories was another way to pass the time. One story told of a frog that could jump long distances. Mark Twain, a young writer from Missouri, heard the tale. He turned it into a short story that he wrote. The short story made him famous.

Because the prospectors spent most of their time searching for gold, they didn't have time to hunt or plant crops. They rarely had fresh meat. Many of them suffered from scurvy, a disease caused by a lack of vitamin C. Scurvy was cured by eating enough fruits and vegetables, but those were in short supply.

Supply trains traveled through the mountains to the camps, but they weren't really trains at all. They were traders with mules that carried packs containing all sorts of supplies and food. The traders exchanged things like axes, shovels, pickles, and onions for gold.

Snow covered the mountains in winter.

The problem with the supply trains was that they couldn't always make it through the mountains. Bad weather and steep, slick trails made the journey difficult.

Miners found that winters in the mountains were much too cold for prospecting. Some miners went to San Francisco for the winter. Many of these men spent lots of money, sure that they would always find more gold.

CHAPTER 4

 LAND OF GOLD

Tiny traces of gold can be found all over the world. A large amount sometimes builds up in one place, as it did in California. How did this happen? Long ago, hot water from volcanoes in California melted gold. The gold washed into cracks in rocks. Over thousands of years, those rocks changed into beds of **quartz**. The quartz contained gold.

As more time passed, wind, water, and ice wore away mountains that contained the quartz. The quartz broke down into sand and gravel. The gold separated from the sand and gravel.

Streams and rivers carried the sand, gravel, and gold along, but the gold dropped to the bottom because it is eight times heavier than sand or gravel. Gold dust and nuggets collected in holes and places where the water slowed, such as behind a big rock in a stream.

Gold mixed with sand and gravel is called **placer gold**. Placer gold was easy to find in the early days of the Gold Rush. The gold nugget that James Marshall found at Sutter's Mill was placer gold.

The first miners didn't really have to work very hard to find gold. They just used pocket knives to get at the placer gold between rocks in rivers and streams. They then used a spoon to scoop out the gold. The miners also dug into the gravel at the bottom of gullies to find pockets of gold mixed with sand. These pockets were called "pay dirt." The miners then put the pay dirt on blankets and shook them gently. The sand blew away. The gold stayed behind on the blankets.

Later, finding placer gold became hard work. Miners began to use water to separate gold from sand and gravel. They called this kind of mining placer mining. The simplest kind of placer mining was known as **panning** for gold. The prospector scooped up gravel, sand, and water from a stream or river. Then he swirled it around in a wash pan, picking out the gravel and letting the water slosh out. The gold was heavier than the sand and water, so it sank to the bottom of the pan and stayed there. The water in the pan washed most of the sand away.

A prospector panning for gold

The prospector then emptied the pan and put the sand and gold in the sun to dry. Later the prospector blew gently to remove the sand.

Panning for gold was similar to the way that the Miwok and Maidu American Indians used watertight baskets to wash gold. These groups of people had known where gold was located for centuries. It had not been valuable to them, so they'd ignored it.

Panning for gold meant long hours squatting beside a river or standing in it. The cold mountain water numbed the prospector's hands and feet. Finding the tiny bits of gold took hours. At night the prospector dried his pan beside the fire. Then he'd look for little bits of gold that might be in the remaining **sediment**.

Some miners used a **cradle** to separate gold from rocks and sand. The cradle didn't rock a baby, but it did rock gold. The cradle had a small wooden box set on top of a larger

Prospectors with a cradle

wooden box. The top box had holes in the bottom of it. The bottom box had ridges to catch gold. The bottom box was set on rockers.

Prospectors liked the cradle because they could wash three or four times more rocks and sand by using it. Three or four times more rocks and sand meant more gold. However, more than one man was needed to use a cradle. A group of three men worked best. One prospector dug up rocks and sand and shoveled them into the top box. Another poured water over the rocks and sand. The third rocked the cradle rapidly to force the water from the bottom box.

Chinese miners using a cradle

The top box trapped the rocks. Gold caught on the ridges of the bottom box while the sand and water washed out.

As more and more prospectors looked for gold, surface gold became harder to find. Prospectors had to figure out new ways to mine. Some built dams to stop water from flowing over a riverbed. Then they could dig for gold in the river bottom. Others lengthened the cradle into a long narrow container that was about 10 feet (3 meters) long. This new device was called a **Long Tom**.

A prospector using a Long Tom

Some of the Long Toms became more than 100 feet (30 meters) long. Miners washed tons of dirt and rocks through the Long Toms. As with the cradle, the gold sank to the bottom. Many prospectors were needed to work the Long Toms, but they could wash much more rocks and sand this way and find more gold.

The Chinese were skilled in mining gold. They came thousands of miles to *Gum San,* or "Gold Mountain," to make their fortune. Because some of the Chinese had mined in other parts of the world, they were more successful than most forty-niners. By using a "Chinese waterwheel," some often found gold in places that other prospectors had left behind. The waterwheel had buckets on a rope for draining streams so that gold could be found more easily.

Mexicans used a machine to crush quartz that contained gold. A mule pulled a log in a circle. The log pulled heavy stones over the quartz, crushing it. Then the prospectors could separate the gold from the quartz.

Some of the forty-niners formed small groups to mine in the earth. They wanted to dig down to the bedrock to reach pockets of gold, and this took a lot of work. Digging down to the bedrock was called **coyote-hole mining**. This kind of mining was named after the holes coyotes dig to make homes. First the prospectors had to dig a hole large enough for men to climb inside.

When they reached the bedrock, they dug tunnels in all directions, trying to find as much gold as they could. Prospectors didn't have much room to move in the tunnels. They usually had to break through rocks and hard-packed sand and gravel.

Coyote-hole mining was dangerous work. Many men did not know how to use timber to keep the hole from caving in. Men were crushed when the sides of the hole gave way and buried them. Coyote-hole mining was popular, though, because it often paid off.

Large amounts of water were needed for many kinds of mining.

In 1850 gold was found in hills away from streams and rivers. This gold was still embedded in **veins** of quartz. Prospectors digging to find gold in quartz began a new kind of mining, **lode mining**. A vein of quartz is called a **lode**. A large vein of quartz is called a **mother lode**. When James Marshall discovered gold at Sutter's Mill, he actually had found the northern end of the Sierra Nevada mother lode. This single vein of gold-bearing quartz stretched south for 120 miles (192 kilometers).

Despite great hardships and failures, some lucky prospectors really did strike it rich. An African-American man named Hector was a cook on a ship that came into San Francisco. He left with the rest of the crew to go to the diggings. He returned with $4,000 in gold. In one month a miner on the Yuba River found 30 pounds of gold in an area 4 feet (3.6 meters) square. At Durgan's Flat, four men took out $12,900 worth of gold in 11 days.

Even more exciting were the large nuggets some people found. One prospector found a large nugget at the edge of a potato patch owned by a man named Holden. The nugget, called the Holden Garden Nugget, weighed 28 pounds!

In 1850 a man at the Carson Hill diggings found a 13-pound nugget lying on the ground. Shortly after, a miner at Carson Hill discovered the largest nugget ever found in California. It weighed 162 pounds and was worth $43,534. That same nugget would be worth almost $1 million today.

George McKnight found a vein of gold that was mined for more than 100 years. Almost 6 million ounces (170 million grams) of gold were taken from this mine run by the Empire-Star Mines. That gold would be worth about $2 billion today.

Gold nuggets

CHAPTER 5

AFTER THE GOLD RUSH

During the beginning of the Gold Rush, the average prospector could make about $15 a day. That is like $338 per day now, but it was not the huge fortune that most dreamed of. By 1852 the average profit was just $6 per day. Most prospectors that made money took it or sent it back home.

Some North American prospectors grew jealous of the success of "foreigners." These prospectors managed to get laws passed that heavily taxed prospectors from other countries. The men from other countries could go home empty-handed, or they could pick another job. Many chose to stay in California and change their way of making a living.

Some of the Chinese opened restaurants and other businesses in San Francisco. Many made their fortune there. Some, like Lee Chew, opened laundries. Lee Chew was 16 years old when he came to California.

A California woman gave him a job washing clothes. At the time, male prospectors thought that washing clothes was "women's work" and wouldn't do it. They slept in their clothes, rarely washing them or changing them. Anyone who did wash the prospectors' clothes for them could make a lot of money. Lee Chew learned English and opened his own successful laundry.

Mining was such hard work that many miners from North America gave up after only a few weeks. Some went back home. Others stayed in California but went back to their old way of making a living. Some figured out other ways to make money.

Mifflin Gibbs founded the first African-American newspaper in San Francisco in 1855. It was called *Mirror of the Times* and was very successful.

To wash clothes, people rubbed them against a washboard.

Gibbs later went on to become the first African-American local judge in the United States.

Levi Strauss made his fortune by supplying the prospectors with denim jeans. When he came to California in 1853, Strauss brought some canvas. He planned to sell this fabric to people who needed tents and wagon covers. Strauss found out that what miners really needed was sturdy work pants.

Strauss began to sell canvas work pants, which sold quickly. He then switched to denim, a thick cotton fabric. The first denim he used was tan. Because Strauss thought the tan color was ugly, he had the denim dyed blue.

In the early 1870s, a tailor named Jacob Davis came to Strauss with an idea. Davis had learned that the pockets of the work pants tore out at the top.

Levi Strauss

Davis came up with the idea of hammering pieces of copper at the tops of the pockets to keep them from ripping. Davis and Strauss became business partners in 1873. Soon the jeans called "Levi's" were the most popular work pants in the West. Levi Strauss and Company grew into a very successful business.

By selling wheelbarrows to miners, John Studebaker also made his fortune in California. When he returned to Indiana, he became the country's biggest wagon maker. Later he changed from making wagons to making cars. His Studebaker car became famous.

Mary Ellen Pleasant had been born a slave but was freed at age nine. She went to school in Boston and then became an active part of the Underground Railroad, which helped slaves escape to freedom. One of the slave owners caught Pleasant helping slaves, so she moved to California. Pleasant arrived in

Mary Ellen Pleasant

California at the beginning of the Gold Rush. She opened a boarding house, where miners could rent rooms and buy meals. Pleasant used the money she made to help African Americans in California.

Luzena Stanley Wilson and her family arrived in Sacramento, California, in 1849. One day she was baking biscuits over an open fire. A stranger offered her a ten-dollar gold piece for the biscuits! Luzena realized that she had a way to make money without going to the diggings. She and her husband sold their oxen and bought a hotel. It was very successful until a flood destroyed it.

Not to be stopped, Wilson opened another hotel and a restaurant. She also started a bank that loaned money to miners. Wilson is famous for lining her mattress with gold dust that miners used to repay her. A fire burned down the hotel and restaurant, but Wilson started again. Her new hotel and restaurant was the only building for miles. Restaurant customers ate off tree stumps. Hotel guests slept on stacks of hay. Other people opened businesses around Wilson's, and they called the area Vacaville. Wilson had started a town with her restaurant and hotel.

John Sutter wasn't as lucky as Luzena Wilson. His workers left his fields and sawmill to find gold, and he lost his land and cattle. His house burned in 1866, so he moved to Pennsylvania. Sutter had nothing to show for the discovery of gold on his land and the years of the Gold Rush.

Sam Brannan wasn't lucky either. Brannan was the fellow who shouted, "Gold from the American River!" while holding up a bottle full of gold dust. He went on to become a successful publisher, real estate dealer, and merchant. However, he lost $6 million in a failed business and died poor.

By 1859 the Gold Rush was over. More than $500 million in California gold had been mined. By today's standards, it would be worth $10 billion. Around $81 million in gold was taken just from the California diggings. The days of the prospectors were over, however. Only large mining companies could get to the remaining gold.

People in San Francisco began to show off their wealth by building mansions, fancy hotels, and theaters. By 1870 San Francisco was the tenth-largest city in the United States, and it was all because of the Gold Rush.

San Francisco in the 1860s

43

Bodie, a California ghost town

San Francisco grew at a fast pace, but some mining towns became ghost towns as the gold supplies grew short. A few of the mining towns, such as Maryville and Placerville, are still around today.

Not many women went to California during the Gold Rush, but they followed in large numbers soon after. When California became a state in 1850, it gave women more freedom than other states. For example, women were allowed to open their own businesses. They also started schools, libraries, and churches.

Although most of the gold was gone by 1860, the forty-niners left their mark. In eleven short years, California went from an untamed territory to a bustling, wealthy state. Today California is still known as the Golden State. The golden poppy is the state flower. And the state motto, "Eureka!" ("I found it!"), reminds us of the amazing years of the Gold Rush.

GLOSSARY

claim (klaym) a piece of land chosen by a prospector

coyote-hole mining (ky OH tee hohl MYN ing) a method of looking for gold in which prospectors dug a deep hole to find gold in bedrock

cradle (KRAY duhl) a wooden box on rockers that was used to separate bits of gold from sand and gravel

diggings (DIG ingz) the areas where people went to dig for gold

expensive (ik SPEN siv) having a high price

forty-niners (FAWR tee NYN uhrz) people, mostly men, who went to California during the Gold Rush

Gold Rush (gohld rush) the period from 1848 to 1859 when people rushed to find gold in California

gullies (GUL eez) narrow ditches cut in the earth by heavy rains or running water

historians (his TAWR ee uhnz) people who study past events

lode (lohd) a vein of quartz

lode mining (LOHD MYN ing) a kind of mining in which people dug in the earth to find gold-bearing quartz

Long Tom (lawng tom) a long trough for washing rocks and sand in order to separate out the gold

mother lode (MUTH uhr lohd) a main lode, or vein, of quartz

nugget (NUG it) a rough lump of gold

panning (PAN ing) sifting sand, dirt, and gravel in a pan of water in order to find gold

placer gold (PLAS uhr gohld) a deposit of gold particles above the ground

prospectors (PROS pek tuhrz) people who looked for gold

quartz (kwawrtz) a hard, clear mineral

sediment (SED uh muhnt) small pieces of things that settle at the bottom of liquid

territory (TER uh tawr ee) an area that is part of the United States but is not a state

treaty (TREE tee) a formal agreement made between two or more countries or groups

veins (vaynz) narrow channels or beds of mineral in rock

wagon train (WAG uhn trayn) a group of covered wagons traveling west together

INDEX